D1333462

ERIC APPLEBY: ZERO TO HERO

D. Worsley

Dan Worsley

ILLUSTRATED BY MARTIN SPORE

ISBN: 978-1515357056

Also by Dan Worsley:

Impossible Tales!

Prologue

Some people are life's winners, successful at everything they attempt, whereas others are downright losers who rarely taste a morsel of success. Most of us experience joyous moments of victory at some point in our lives, but some folk wade through a surging tide of disaster and failure, one mishap quickly following the last.

Eleven-year-old Eric Appleby fitted perfectly into the failure category. He was the type of person who only occasionally succeeded. Whether it was bombing another test or failing to make friends, he had lurched from one disaster to another and left a trail of broken dreams and dashed hopes in his wake.

Despite all his failures, Eric soldiered on and never threw in the towel. Which is just as well, because as you are about to discover, when Eric finally tasted his moment of glory, it was in the most unimaginable circumstances. That inbuilt resilience served him well, and his brave, selfless actions changed his life, and the lives of those around him, forever.

ERIC   DAD

IVANA   HEAD

Chapter 1

The chaotic playground at Linkton School was a hive of activity. Children buzzed around, some charging after a bouncing football like bees around a honey pot, while others flailed skipping ropes or waved tennis racquets as they swatted at balls rocketing from one end of the yard to the other. The cacophony of excited voices was punctuated only by the occasional whistle or Mr Watt's raised voice as he patrolled the yard like some kind of power-crazed prison warden. He was constantly on the lookout for any offenders, who then received a stern ticking off or a boring lecture about the school rules if he happened to catch them committing such shocking crimes as venturing onto the grass or daring to jump in the puddles.

Every child appeared to be enjoying their fifteen minutes of freedom away from the classroom and the chance to take in the fresh air, despite the day being cool and somewhat chilly. Everyone, that was, apart from one young boy who was tucked away at the end of the yard, sitting alone on a muddy footprint-covered bench.

He cut a lonely, isolated figure and his brown, greasy hair blew in the gentle breeze as he sat with his arms tightly folded. The metal zip of the boy's parka coat was pulled right up to his chin so that he could play with it between his chapped, sore-looking lips. A dot-to-dot puzzle of scattered freckles covered the pale, nearly translucent-looking skin on his face. Heavy, black rings below his eyes were evidence of too many late nights and a distinct lack of quality sleep.

Daydreaming and staring into oblivion, he was rhythmically swinging his black shoes back and forth, scuffing the heavily worn soles on the tarmac. The gaping holes in the knees of his trousers demonstrated the daily battering they had endured since they'd been purchased many months ago from the charity shop in town. The fact that they sat hoisted high above his sock tops signalled they were now clearly a few sizes smaller than this lanky eleven-year-old actually required. Unfortunately, the chances of him getting a new pair any time soon were slim to non-existent.

Eric Appleby was different to everyone else. Or at least that was how he was made to feel by his peers at Linkton. While others played happily among their friendship groups, Eric lived a solitary existence, blowing around life like a discarded crisp bag on a breezy day. He'd tried his best to make friends and talk to the other children, but it just seemed that he wasn't cut out for friendships and all his attempts had ended in failure. He didn't like sports and that was a major stumbling block.

He had no clue what to say when a conversation started up about football and unfortunately, 99.9% of the boys in his class talked incessantly about kicking a ball around or some blokes they had watched playing the game on television. Eric decided that if you didn't speak the footy language it was virtually impossible to crack the friendship code.

In fact, talking with others generally just wasn't Eric's thing and he was left feeling awkward and out of place. "There's no company as good as your own," his dad constantly advised him, clearly from first-hand experience judging by his own lack of friends. Eric thought the advice seemed very reasonable, and despite his class teacher's best attempts to pair him up with most of the children in his class, he'd decided to keep himself to himself.

As Mr Watt blew the life out of his whistle, Eric wearily hauled himself from his seat and let out a huge yawn. He began to trudge across the yard, merging with the mass of children who funnelled through the double doors and headed back to class. Outside, Mr Watt was vigorously blowing his whistle at a group of younger boys who had decided their football match required extra time beyond the statutory fifteen minutes.

Sighing and frowning at the thought of a double maths session which would undoubtedly bring more red crosses than ticks, but grateful for the warmth of being indoors again, Eric reluctantly headed to class.

Chapter 2

"It's just not good enough!" roared Rodney Mason, the Headteacher of Linkton School, as he vented his anger and frustration at the line of overall-wearing adults who stood silently in his office, heads bowed. Each wisely avoided eye contact with the enraged Head for fear of receiving a severe tongue-lashing. "I expect this school to be clean and tidy and I pay you good money to do that. Yet day in, day out I have complaints about dirty toilets, bins which haven't been emptied and corridors strewn with litter." Scanning the line, he waited for a response like a hungry lion preparing to seize a helpless, passing wildebeest and rip it to shreds.

After what seemed like an eternity in which the only sound was the loud ticking of the clock on the wall, one of the line-up broke their silence.

"We just don't have enough time and there aren't enough of us," said a thick-set, heavily tattooed man in a wavering voice strained with nerves and trepidation.

"You don't have enough time? Absolute rubbish!" bellowed Mr Mason. Purple veins bulged and pulsed on his huge bald head and his wire-rimmed glasses jumped about on his red nose. "If you spent less time chatting, reading trashy magazines and sending texts, I think you'd find you had more than enough time!" The four cleaners stood in silence again. No reply. No reaction. "Well I've had enough," he continued. "I'm serving you all with your notice. Start looking for other jobs because at the end of the week, you're all sacked!"

The two men and two women visibly sagged as the shock of losing their jobs began to sink in. Then a tall woman with blonde hair and dangling, loopy earrings mustered up the courage to speak.

"The school will be in a right state without us," she protested, trying a last-ditch attempt to reverse the Head's decision. "Just imagine how much worse things will get with no cleaners at all."

Mr Mason walked to his office door and opened it. "You don't need to worry about that," he said with a smirk. "I've found some cleaners who'll do a substantially better job than you lot have been doing and at a much cheaper price too. There's nothing else left to say. Please go and get on with what I pay you to do for the rest of the week." Gesturing towards the open door, he ushered the disconsolate figures out before closing it behind them.

Returning to his desk, he slumped his huge frame on his black leather chair and broadly smiled as he picked up a steaming-hot cup of coffee in one hand, and a handful of biscuits from a tin on his desk in the other. Stuffing the custard creams into his mouth and showering crumbs down onto his suit jacket and trousers, he began to noisily slurp his coffee, happy in the knowledge that he was the boss and the boss was always right. Sacking a few lazy cleaners had so far been the highlight of his day, plus he had a far better idea in mind. Rodney Mason had a cunning plan up his sleeve which would make his life a whole lot easier.

Chapter 3

"Hi, Dad," Eric called as he walked into the dingy flat. Pushing the door closed behind him and still awaiting some sort of response, he dumped his school bag in the hallway and made his way to the tiny kitchen at the rear of the flat. He was met by the sight of tower blocks of dirty plates and food-encrusted cutlery littering every available surface.

He felt his stomach rumbling and headed for the cupboard in the vain hope of discovering something edible. An out-of-date jar of mustard and half a bag of dry pasta twirls dashed his hopes completely. The cupboard had held his best chance of food and, not fancying the prospect of nibbling on the scouring pads from under the sink, Eric abandoned the search and headed back to the lounge to find his dad.

Eric found him slumped in the chair in the corner of the lounge, fast asleep. The dozing man's hairy belly peeped out from the gap between his T-shirt and tracksuit bottoms. His wiry moustache was twitching and wiggling as he dreamed. Dad's shaven head was tilted to one side. His mouth was wide open and a single string of drool dribbled from one side of the cavernous entry and onto the shoulder of his faded top. What a beautiful sight! Snoring loudly in competition with the television which was playing to itself, Dad was clearly in a deep slumber.

On the television, an old woman with pencilled-on eyebrows, wearing a multicoloured cardigan, eagerly awaited the valuation on a pair of ugly-looking dog-shaped cups from the expert on 'Antique Hunters'. She was clearly hoping for some extra cash to bump up her weekly pension and was hanging on the professional's every word and praying for a bumper payday.

"Dad!" bellowed Eric, causing the man to sit bolt upright and wave his arms as if fighting off an invisible intruder. The racing guide perched on his portly belly was sent flying up in the air.

"Who? What? When? Where?" frantically questioned the confused man, who was clearly still half asleep and desperately trying to work out where he was and who had so rudely awakened him. Rubbing his eyes, he stared at Eric, unsure whether his son was real or part of a dream.

"Another busy day?" Eric asked sarcastically. He gazed down at the racing guide which had now joined the crumbs and fluff on the worn carpet. Looking back at his dad's face, Eric instantly regretted the comment.

Sighing deeply, Dad looked his son in the eye. "You know I'm looking for work," he quietly replied. "There just isn't much about at the minute." Trying to come up with a positive, he added, "I did spot a job at the rubber glove factory. I reckon I've got a chance you know."

Nodding and forcing a smile, Eric patted his dad on the shoulder which wasn't coated in cold drool. "Brilliant. I reckon that job's got your name on it," he said in a hopeful, but not entirely convincing manner, before changing the direction of the conversation to dinner.

"Nip to the shop and get a loaf and a tin of beans," instructed Dad as he handed Eric the handful of loose change – the sum total of his wealth until his benefits money was paid at the end of the week. "We'll have some food and conquer that mountain of washing up. Then I reckon it's film time. What do you say?"

For the first time that day, Eric felt a flicker of excitement. Not about beans on toast for tea for the third time that week, and most definitely not about the colossal pile of washing up. Grabbing the change and heading out of the flat to the corner shop, he smiled to himself at the prospect of an evening with his dad and a film, just the two of them. Perfect!

Chapter 4

After the famished pair had devoured their hastily thrown-together dinner and worked their way through the gargantuan stack of washing up, they made a half-hearted attempt at tidying the lounge. This mainly involved moving piles of junk from one spot to another and was made worthwhile when Eric found a £1 coin under a stack of old faded newspapers that, judging by the dates, had been waiting to be tidied for a good few months.

"So what do you fancy watching tonight?" asked Dad as he rifled through the box of DVDs perched on his knee. "How about 'Ultimate Action Adventure 5' or 'Calling Out For A Hero'? They both look fantastic and only cost me twenty pence each from the charity shop. They're both classics. Action films these days aren't a patch on what they used to be," he added enthusiastically.

Since Mum passed away three years ago, the movies Eric and his dad watched tended to be a lot more action-based. Mum used to love a good romantic comedy but the men of the house preferred edge-of-the-seat drama rather than stories of people falling in love. Eric and his dad had spent countless hours watching endless supplies of cheap DVDs which Dad picked up from jumble sales and charity shops. They had provided many cheap nights of entertainment.

Eric desperately missed his mum, although he'd gradually adjusted to life without her. Nearly three years on and a single day didn't pass without him quietly reminiscing about the amazing times they'd had together. The love they felt for each other would never die. Mum may have been taken away from him far too soon but the memories she'd left behind would stay forever in Eric's heart.

"I've heard great things about both films," said Eric. "You choose. As long as there's plenty of action, I'm not bothered!"

Placing the box of films on the threadbare carpet, Dad removed the DVD from the case and gave it a clean on his filthy T-shirt before pushing the disc into the player. Excitedly grabbing the remote, he joined Eric back on the sofa and after a few clicks, the movie began.

For the next hour and a half, the pair sat staring at the television as if hypnotised or under a spell. They whooped and clapped as they watched a series of high-speed car chases, shoot-outs and all manner of far-fetched action set pieces.

"What an awesome flick! That's got to be one of the best he's made," said Dad as he pressed the off button when the final credits began to roll.

"Troy Randall is the best action hero ever and that was a classic performance," replied Eric. "He just knows how to sort out the bad guys! I love the way he uses all those ingenious methods of catching them. Who else could use just a brush and a ball of string to take out four baddies?"

Nodding in agreement, Dad knelt down, ejected the disc and placed it back in the case before returning it to the stash of other movies in the cardboard box. "Yeah, Troy Randall is definitely the ultimate action hero," said Dad as he yawned loudly. "Right young Eric, it's time for bed. You've got school in the morning and I need to be at the Job Centre nice and early to follow up on that position at the rubber glove factory."

Heading upstairs, the pair called it a night. Eric pulled on his ill-fitting pyjamas before snuggling down under the smelly duvet which was more than overdue for a boil wash. With a bit of luck, his dreams would be filled with action and adventure just like Troy Randall's films, rather than the impending gloom of another day at school which would undoubtedly be jam-packed with yet more glorious failures.

Chapter 5

"Miss Da Cash is here for your 9am meeting about the new cleaners," said Mrs Anderson, the school secretary as she placed the Head's morning coffee on his table. He didn't even say thank you, just grunted an undecipherable reply and nodded, then picked up the cup and noisily slurped away. Mrs Anderson left the room, muttering under her breath.

As Miss Da Cash walked in, Rodney Mason was awestruck. Her jet-black hair looked as if it had been spray-painted on. Her fringe was perfect and her clothes were smart and business-like. She wore skyscraper stilettos that clicked and clacked on the tiled office floor. The woman radiated an air of confidence and self-belief which filled the room.

"Good morning, Mr Mason," she said. "It's nice to finally put a face to the voice after all of our phone calls."

The Head placed his cup on the table and wiped his mouth with his handkerchief before reaching out his other hand and was surprised at the firm handshake he received. "An absolute pleasure to finally meet you, Miss Da Cash," he said. "Please call me Rodney. No need at all for such formalities."

"I agree completely, I insist that you call me Ivana," she replied as she released her vice-like grip on the Head's hand. "Let's get down to business."

Rodney Mason pushed his office door shut before returning to his desk, where Ivana Da Cash had already lifted a pile of paperwork from her case and laid it out. The Head leaned forward, lowering his voice to barely a whisper and began to nervously speak. "You do understand that anything we discuss is highly confidential, don't you? If the truth behind my motives for sacking our cleaners was to come out, it could cause real problems for me."

Ivana smiled and gently patted the back of the Head's outstretched hand, before looking him in the eye. "You can trust me completely, Rodney," she said.

Forcing a half-hearted smile, Rodney Mason hung on Ivana Da Cash's every word as she explained how her four state-of-the-art robotic cleaners would work twice as hard as the lazy layabouts who were currently doing the job and would shortly be looking for alternative

employment. He grinned as she revealed Linkton School would be the first in the world to employ these futuristic creations, bringing huge amounts of free publicity and raising the profile of the school. He rubbed his hands at the thought of magazine interviews and unlimited airtime on the television and radio.

"Just to make it clear, you don't want a penny for these robotic cleaners for the first three months?" said Rodney Mason.

"That's correct," Ivana replied. "It's purely a trial period to see if you're happy with their performance."

"Marvellous," he replied as he thought about the money that would be saved from sacking the cleaners and the free service he was being offered. "Are they completely safe? I don't want them blowing up or causing any injuries. Parents these days will sue for anything. If one of their little darlings is run over by an out-of-control robotic cleaner, it'd cost me a fortune in legal bills!"

"They've been thoroughly tested in my factory and have passed rigorous examinations and fulfilled specific safety requirements. They'll be programmed to do all of the jobs your human staff already do. You can rest assured everything will be fine," said Ivana as she reached out and gently patted the back of Rodney's hand again.

Delving into her handbag, Ivana Da Cash removed a large brown envelope which she pushed across the desk. Smiling broadly, she nodded towards the envelope before leaning back in her chair. The Head looked from the envelope to Ivana and back again, then picked up the package and tore it open to reveal a thick bundle of cash. At first, his brain couldn't compute how many £50 notes were tightly packed together.

"What's this? Is this all for me?" squeaked the shell-shocked man. His eyes bulged and his mind whirled.

Ivana Da Cash breathed deeply before smiling. "It's all for you, my dear Rodney. Every penny of the £75,000. Don't worry though. Nobody will know about it. It will be our secret. Just think of it as a 'little thank you' for being part of this exciting project and allowing me to trial my robotic cleaners in your wonderful school," she said.

A mixture of excitement and fear surged through the stunned Headteacher's body. Ivana Da Cash was attempting to bribe him in the hope of getting the contract for the robotic cleaners. Rodney Mason knew that if he accepted the money and was then found out he would be sacked and thrown into jail. On the other hand, this money would go a long way to setting him up for life. It would allow him to retire much earlier than he had planned. No more misbehaving kids causing him endless problems. No more moaning teachers complaining about their jobs and giving him constant headaches. No more school inspectors telling him how badly his school was performing.

As he slipped the cash back into the envelope and placed it in his desk drawer, the decision was made. In his mind, Rodney desperately tried to justify his actions as he signed the numerous pieces of paper which Ivana had laid out on his desk. The deal was sealed. Ivana Da Cash would use Linkton School to trial her robotic cleaners and he would instantly become rich beyond his wildest dreams! He rubbed his hands together, dreaming about all the luxuries he could buy with his ill-gotten gains, and watched as Ivana packed away the paperwork.

"Nice doing business with you," she said before shaking Rodney's hand and leaving. On her way out, she smiled a self-satisfied smile. How easily the greedy fool had fallen for her plan! Stage one of her operation had gone off without a hitch.

Chapter 6

The diminutive Miss Gregory stood at the front of the class, waiting for silence. She glanced at the classroom clock before unleashing a deafeningly impressive roar which boomed and thundered around the room. Although Eric disliked school, he liked his class teacher, mainly because she didn't take any messing. In his book that was an essential quality of a good teacher and somewhat eased the pain of the daily grind.

With the class finally sitting in silence, Miss Gregory spoke. "Today's lesson will be cut short as we have to attend a whole school assembly."

"What's it about?" blurted out Hanif, earning him an icy stare. He slowly sank down in his seat, his question unanswered.

"Right class, let's get into some sort of orderly queue rather than the shambles which you usually call a line," instructed Miss Gregory.

As the rest of the class sorted themselves out, Eric tagged on at the back. It was his usual spot and a key part of his classroom responsibility. He'd been desperate for a class job, and when Miss Gregory finally awarded him the honour of being 'Energy Conservation Monitor', he couldn't hide his delight. In his heart, Eric thought his role was as good as an MBE or some other high-ranking award. Miss Gregory had made a big thing about presenting Eric with his laminated cardboard badge in front of the class. She had made him feel like he played an integral part in the day-to-day running of the classroom. He felt like a big player in the grand scheme of things.

In reality, Eric's job was to turn off the classroom light switch. Nothing more, nothing less. It was however, a role in which he took great pride and during the five months of the new school year, he hadn't once forgotten to fulfil his duties. He may have bombed fourteen maths tests, failed to spell any words correctly on his spelling tests and not succeeded in making a single friend, but when it came to switching off the lights, nobody could rival Eric Appleby! Flicking off the switch, he followed the line as they filed into the hall and sat down on the orange plastic chairs. The hundreds of children waited for the assembly to begin.

Eric looked across the stage to see Mr Mason pacing around like a caged lion. Alongside him sat a smartly dressed woman in a pinstripe business suit, whom Eric didn't recognise. Next to her was a figure covered by a sheet. Eric could make out the shape of a head and shoulders and he guessed the mysterious individual underneath was around six feet tall. Was it some famous celebrity? he wondered. He smiled at the thought of Troy Randall hiding under the sheet and then instantly dismissed the idea. Things like that didn't happen in real life. Unfortunately action heroes were restricted to television screens and didn't turn up at schools, especially not Linkton.

"Right students, quiet please. I have an extremely exciting announcement to make today," said Mr Mason, through a black microphone which he gripped tightly. The chatter died away. "As some of you may be aware, we are having a restructure with our cleaning staff and today I can reveal some exciting news. The new cleaners at Linkton will not be humans."

The Head's comments prompted a burst of excited chatter. Eric frowned and shook his head. How could people who work in a school not be human? It didn't make any sense!

"Quiet, please. Quiet!" urged the Head as he tried to extinguish the wildfire conversations which had broken out around the hall. Eric watched as Mr Mason turned and gestured towards the smartly dressed woman sitting behind him. She stood, flicked back her jet-black hair and made her way across to the mysterious covered figure. The audience fell silent and awaited the big reveal.

Passing the microphone to the woman, Mr Mason reluctantly stepped aside and allowed all of the audience's attention to focus on her. The anticipation was now at fever-pitch and everyone in the hall was desperate to see what was under the sheet.

"My name is Ivana Da Cash," announced the woman in a confident, authoritative voice. "I am the managing director of IDC Robotics and I'm proud to be here today to reveal your new cleaners, which my company will be manufacturing and supplying." As she spoke, Mr Mason gazed adoringly at her like a love-struck teenager. "Your new cleaners will be state-of-the-art robotic creations controlled and programmed by myself." Taking hold of one corner of the sheet, she paused in a deliberate attempt to crank up the expectation. "Linkton School, I present to you the future of robotic technology!"

The big reveal left the children temporarily stunned. Standing on the stage was a life-size robot. The creation was approximately six feet tall and the first thing Eric noticed were the glowing blue eyes which shone like beacons. It was neither male nor female looking and made from gleaming, polished metal. Different shaped buttons and flashing bulbs were dotted around its body and there was what looked like a control panel on its chest which had all manner of dials and switches mounted on it.

Eric tried to take it all in as Ivana Da Cash flicked a switch on the robot's control panel and it came to life. It began to move around the stage, clanking along, before stopping and turning to face the audience. The robotic cleaner raised an arm and began to wave to the baffled onlookers. The children stood up and waved back, whooping in enthralled delight.

Every child apart from Eric Appleby, that is. He watched suspiciously, carefully taking in what he was seeing, not blinded by the razzmatazz which had been caused by the sensational robotic reveal. Eric looked past the machine, which was now moving backward and forward while waving a duster around and squirting polish from a canister. He focused his attention on Ivana Da Cash who was standing in the background wearing a self-satisfied grin. Something didn't feel right, and Eric had an unsettling feeling in the pit of his stomach.

Chapter 7

"Guess what!" yelled Dad as Eric trudged in through the front door. "I got the job. I'm now an employee at the rubber glove factory. I've finally got a job!" He swept up Eric and hugged him tightly.

"That's great news, Dad," replied Eric as he broke free from his dad's bear hug and smiled with delight. "I'm so proud of you. I knew you'd get work sooner rather than later."

"We definitely need to celebrate," said Dad. "How about we raid the emergency money in the biscuit tin and treat ourselves to sausage and chips from the chippy? Let's have a pickled egg too. Come on young Eric, we need to mark this momentous occasion. What do you say?"

"Sounds perfect," replied Eric, as he excitedly made his way to the kitchen. After pulling the lid from the rusty biscuit tin and removing the crisp £5 note which was lying at the bottom among the crumbs, he headed off. "I'll be back in a bit," he called.

Eric and his dad feasted like kings that night and they both appreciated the rare feeling of having a full stomach. Compared to the scraped-together meals they'd endured lately, sausage and chips with a pickled egg felt like a slap-up meal produced in a high-class restaurant by a world-famous chef.

Leaning back in his chair, Dad massaged his swollen belly and let out a thunderous burp, sending the pair into fits of giggles. "Is it Troy time?" asked Dad waving his foot in the direction of the box containing the ever-growing collection of DVDs.

Sliding from the sofa, Eric went to the DVD box and rifled through the contents before brandishing his choice in Dad's direction.

"That'll do nicely, young Eric," said Dad. "Get it on."

Eric inserted the disc into the player before returning to the sofa. Lying down, he grabbed the remote and started the movie. Before long, Dad was snoring noisily in his chair; the exertion of his job interview had clearly tired him out. Eric watched on alone, basking in a warm glow of happiness.

Eric fell fast asleep too, long before the final credits had rolled. Sickening odours filled the room, produced by the slumbering pair who blasted out a series of pickled egg-tainted trumps. But there was an air of contentment in the Appleby household. Today's job news had made it a diamond of a day – and in the life of Eric Appleby, days like this had to be savoured as they didn't come along very often.

Chapter 8

For the next few days, Eric watched suspiciously as the robotic cleaners went about their business at Linkton. He watched as one robot emptied the bin on the yard, even bending down to pick up a discarded crisp wrapper. He thought their glowing electric blue eyes had a sinister look to them. Eric's gut feeling still remained but he felt like he was the only person who didn't think these robotic creations were the greatest thing to ever happen to Linkton School. It was all too good to be true and Eric was sure it was only a matter of time before things took a turn for the worse. Dad had always called him a young cynic, but this time he felt that his cynicism would be proved right – and soon.

Meanwhile, Rodney Mason was living the dream! All his Christmases had come at once. He'd featured on national television many times and camera crews were a regular feature at the school. Eric spotted him on the yard as he daydreamed through the window during a lesson.

The Head was chatting to a film crew with his arm around the shoulders of one of the robots. He'd been catapulted from obscurity to near-celebrity status and Mr Mason was revelling in his fifteen minutes of fame. His head seemed to be growing bigger by the day!

As Eric was sitting alone in the canteen eating his lunch, he watched one of the robots make its way to a spillage. A little girl's cup of juice had wobbled off her tray during the tricky balancing act she had to perform between being served and sitting down. The robot mopped up the mess and even placed a sign over the wet area to alert students to the slippery hazard. After placing the mop back in the bucket, it turned around and trundled off before disappearing through the double doors at the end of the hall.

Eric put his plate, bowl and cutlery onto his tray and handed them in before making his way to the ICT suite. This was his safe haven, somewhere he could go at lunch break to avoid the feeling of being the odd one out in the wilderness of the playground. Technically, he shouldn't really have been allowed in but Miss Aziz, the IT technician, had taken pity on him and was willing to bend the rules in his case. She'd seen Eric floating around like a fallen leaf on an autumnal day and had offered him the chance to spend his lunches in the computer suite. He would often do jobs for her, including setting up for the afternoon sessions, loading paper into the printers or replacing empty ink cartridges. Eric lapped up the added responsibility and so far it was one of the few parts of school, along with his light switch duties, he hadn't managed to stuff up. He had also picked up some useful computer programming skills which Miss Aziz shared with him while she sat and ate her lunch.

When there were no jobs to do or Miss Aziz was busy, Eric entertained himself by cruising the internet and watching trailers of classic Troy Randall films on sites his dad had discovered during hours of net surfing at the local library while he was 'looking for a job'. Clicking the mouse button, Eric smiled as a clip popped up on the screen.

"Just got to nip out, Eric," said Miss Aziz as she left the room, leaving him on his own to enjoy some brief clips of Troy Randall sorting out the bad guys in his own unique way. The scene Eric was currently watching involved Troy taking out two bad guys using only a hairdryer and a box of table tennis balls. The guy was incredible!

Eric was happy in his own little world until he heard the school public address system buzz into life.

A voice he had heard only days earlier began to speak. "Everyone in the school, adults and children, please move towards the main hall immediately," instructed Ivana Da Cash.

Eric was baffled and presumed it was some kind of emergency drill practice. Pushing the swivel chair back before standing up, he went to the window and parted the dusty blinds to look out onto the yard below. What he saw made him realise that the announcement was very real. The robotic cleaners were no longer picking up rubbish or tidying the school grounds. They were shepherding the children across the yard towards the hall like sheep dogs herding a flock of sheep into a pen. Eric could see the pupils were as baffled as he was. Some children turned and asked questions to their robotic shepherds, while others were shaking their heads and looking confused. Generally, they appeared to be calm and following the instructions given by Ivana Da Cash via the speaker system.

As he backed away from the window, the speaker system crackled into life again. "Don't attempt to hide or escape. If you do as I ask, everyone will be fine," she instructed in what sounded like a harsher tone. "Failure to follow my instructions will result in severe repercussions."

Eric's limited vocabulary didn't extend to knowing what the final word of that sentence meant, but judging by the rest of the announcements, one thing remained clear; Eric's feelings of unease about Ivana Da Cash and her fleet of robotic cleaners appeared to be fully justified.

Chapter 9

Eric made his way over to the classroom door and peeked through the small glass window. The corridor was unusually quiet compared to the usual hustle and bustle of lunchtimes. He stuck his head out to check the coast was clear, then stepped into the deserted corridor and made his way towards the hall. Something was telling him things were amiss and he wanted to find out exactly what was happening.

Passing one deserted classroom after another, he neared the hall. He crept along the freshly polished walkway and pushed his body tightly against the corridor wall. Children's voices echoed around the hall.

Suddenly the voices fell silent and Ivana Da Cash began to speak. "Thank you so much for complying with my instructions. If you continue to co-operate, everyone will be just fine. We do not intend to hurt any of you, unless you force us to do otherwise. When I have got what I want, you will all be released safely and this whole episode will have a happy ending."

Eric tried to process what he had just heard. This was a kidnap situation! This Da Cash woman and her fleet of robots had captured the children and staff. Carefully shuffling nearer the windows at the rear of the hall, Eric peeped between the curtains, trying his best to remain out of sight.

The children were sitting on the wooden floor in what appeared to be class groups and the teachers were assembled at the front. Ivana Da Cash was standing on the stage and the four robots were guarding the exits, one on each door. The mood had clearly changed and some of the children were now whispering nervously, while others sat and silently watched what was going on. The teachers huddled together around Mr Mason, who was wearing an expression of deep concern.

"Teachers," instructed Ivana Da Cash, "complete the registers. Inform me of any students who are missing."

The teachers dispersed around the room and

stood by their classes. Calling out the names, they marked the sheets which they had been given before returning to the stage and handing them to Ivana Da Cash, who snatched them back without as much as a thank you.

Eric watched Miss Gregory, who was the last to return her register, as she made her way to the front of the hall and handed in the sheet. He could see her talking to Ivana Da Cash before the clearly agitated woman snatched the register from Miss Gregory's hand.

"Silence! Silence!" Ivana shrieked even though the children were barely speaking. "We have a problem and I despise problems! Problems give me headaches and I hate headaches! There's a child missing. Does anyone know where Eric Appleby is?" Nobody in the room reacted.

Eric's blood ran cold as he watched the events unfold, even though he wanted to make a break for freedom. Ivana Da Cash picked up the microphone from the table on the stage. The school speaker system burst into life again.

"Eric Appleby. Can you hear me, Eric Appleby? I'd like you to make your way to the hall immediately," she instructed in a stern and commanding voice.

There was no way in a million years that Eric was going to accept her invitation. Instead, he tiptoed away from the hall towards the main entrance and pushed the door. It was locked. Moving further down the corridor, he tried the emergency exit but that was securely locked too. Whatever was happening, it was well organised and there was no way of escape. Linkton School was in lockdown!

As Eric stood in the corridor, pondering his next move, he heard the hall door creak open and to his horror one of the robots emerged. It stopped in its tracks and slowly rotated its mechanised head in Eric's direction. The robot's piercing blue eyes were firmly fixed on Eric who felt like he was glued to the floor. Suddenly, the robot swivelled its polished body and started to move towards him, its heavy metal feet clanking on the hard floor.

Chapter 10

"What on earth are you doing?" boomed Mr Mason. He glared at Ivana Da Cash, who was prowling around the stage like a hungry tiger. "You can't possibly think that you can get away with this ludicrous plan!"

She gave the Headteacher a glare of utter contempt and sniggered. "I suggest you keep quiet, Rodney or else I might just let it slip about that little cash bonus."

The Head backed away, muttering under his breath while contemplating his next move. She had him backed into a corner and he was desperately regretting the moment he'd accepted the bribe. "What do you possibly hope to achieve from all of this?" he asked, moving the conversation away from anything which could incriminate him or reveal his part in the plan.

Ivana rubbed her hands together and smiled like a sly fox as she scanned the groups of children sitting in clusters around the hall. "I guess we'll see how much the Mayor of Linkton values the students of his town. If he pays me what I want, everyone goes home happy. Simple."

"You're crazy! You can't get away with such a ludicrous plan. I won't let you!" ranted the Head.

"Oh sit down, you foolish man," hissed Ivana as her patience snapped, a darker, more sinister tone in her voice. "I'll do exactly what I want and nobody, including you, will stop me!"

The hall fell silent. All eyes were fixed on Ivana Da Cash as she strutted across the stage, her high-heeled shoes clicking and clacking with each step. "The Mayor has been contacted and if he meets my demands, this'll all end happily. If he hands over the cash, I'll send you all home safely. If not I'll have to take alternative action. Trust me, you need to pray that he comes up with the goods. The other option is much more painful!" she said in a threatening tone.

The hall was filled with a dark, foreboding silence as she click-clacked her way down the steps and strutted out among the children. Some huddled together and offered comfort to each other, while others sat in quiet contemplation of their predicament. The teachers sat among the pupils and offered reassuring smiles, hiding their uncertainty.

Ivana stopped by a girl with long blonde hair and smiled pleasantly at the child, who nervously smiled back. Then, without warning, the woman reached down and firmly grabbed a handful of the girl's hair, snapping her head back and causing the innocent child to yelp loudly. The children and staff gasped in shock. "Please don't think I'm making idle threats," Ivana said calmly, still clutching the girl's long blonde locks. The child whimpered and tears streamed down her freckled cheeks. "I'm used to getting what I want and if it means causing a little pain and suffering along the way, then so be it." Letting go of the young girl's hair, she strutted back to the stage, leaving the poor child to be comforted by Miss Gregory. This spite-filled woman was clearly willing to go to any extremes, including inflicting pain on children, if it meant that she was to achieve her goal. The pupils' minds ran wild at the thought of the horrifying measures she was willing to use.

At the back of the hall, Rodney Mason sat, sobbing softly as he cradled his bald head in his hands. The repercussions of the corrupt deal which he'd struck with this wicked woman had finally dawned on him. He was in over his head and his selfish, money-driven actions had put everyone at Linkton School in grave danger.

Chapter 11

As he thundered down the corridor, Eric didn't need to check if the robotic cleaner was in pursuit. The clanking metal footsteps which echoed down the corridor told him that it was hot on his heels!

As he turned a corner, Eric flung open the classroom door to his right and darted inside before carefully closing it behind him. Seeking cover, he squeezed into the tight space under the teacher's desk. His heart thumped and pounded like a drum as adrenaline surged and powered through his system. He listened intently as the metallic footsteps made their way to the classroom door before they stopped dead.

Eric gulped as the door handle began to lower. The door creaked open and he could make out the robot from its heavy metal boots which clanked into the room before it came to a stop. Eric tried to quieten his ragged breathing while keeping his focus on his robotic hunter. He could hear the buzzing and whirring of the inner workings of the machine in the silence of the room. After momentarily pausing, the robotic predator turned and headed out again. Eric gasped and sucked in as much air as he could before cautiously sliding out from his hiding space.

He tried to take it all in. It seemed he was the only one in the school who'd not been corralled into the hall at lunch. He had two options. He could try to escape from the school grounds and get help, but that would be incredibly risky and virtually impossible as the building was locked down. Even if he did get outside, it would involve crossing the yard and most probably being spotted and captured by Da Cash's fiendishly mechanised creations. There was no cover between the exit doors and the main gates; he would be a sitting duck and easy prey.

"What would Troy Randall do?" Eric whispered to himself. After sitting and pondering his options for a few moments, he realised exactly what Troy would do if he were in a similar situation. Eric's ultimate action hero wouldn't run away or hide;

he'd deal with it – because Troy never allowed the baddies to triumph. He wouldn't let some metallic monstrosities and a power-crazed woman come out on top. No way!

For years, Eric had been a complete nobody at Linkton but he sensed that this was his moment to shine. He wasn't much good at maths or making friends, his spelling was terrible and he couldn't dribble a football without falling over. But Eric Appleby knew that this was his golden opportunity to become a real-life action hero.

Chapter 12

Clutching the register for Eric's class, Ivana Da Cash ran her finger down the list and stopped at his name. She momentarily tapped her fingertip on it while considering her next move.

"Silence!" she suddenly shrieked. The low-level, nervy chatter died down and the staff and children watched and waited. "Where's Eric Appleby? If anybody knows where this kid might be, speak now."

Hesitantly raising her hand, Miss Aziz awaited her opportunity to speak. Ivana Da Cash cast her eyes across the hall and spotted the trembling woman but paused to prolong the wait, before finally giving her permission to speak. "He was working in the ICT suite when I left him. Don't hurt him," pleaded Miss Aziz.

Ivana Da Cash processed the teacher's response in silence. "Oh dear, I think we'd better go out and find poor Eric. We don't want him missing out on all the fun do we?" she said sarcastically. "I wondered where Unit 4 had disappeared to. He must have spotted our missing boy and gone to retrieve him. I'm sure he'll be returned safe and sound, but just to make sure I'll send some assistance."

Precariously tottering down the steps on her high heels, she click-clacked her way across the hall. The children cowered away either side of her, clearing a pathway for her to strut through.

She set off towards the robot at the rear of the hall, but suddenly reached out and snatched a pair of glasses from a boy within grabbing distance. The black-rimmed spectacles fell to the wooden floor and she ground the point of her right stiletto heel into one of the lenses. The glass cracked and shattered. The poor child could only squint in silence at the act of spiteful bullying. Ivana Da Cash cackled at the boy who was now beginning to cry. "Didn't see that coming, did you?" she quipped.

She reached the robot at the rear of the hall. It turned to face the woman, awaiting instructions.

"Unit 1, go out and assist Unit 4 to bring this child in," she firmly instructed. "This wasn't part of the plan. I won't have some troublesome kid getting in my way. Use whatever force necessary to bring him in." It immediately wheeled around and made its way out of the hall, leaving Ivana Da Cash with the two remaining robots to guard the captives and prevent any escape attempts.

Turning to the staff and children, she smiled broadly. "I greatly look forward to meeting our missing friend."

Chapter 13

Eric perched on the teacher's chair in the darkness of the deserted classroom and pondered his next move. He knew there were four robots plus Ivana Da Cash, so it was five versus one. The odds were stacked against him, but Eric had a steely determination to at the very least, give them a run for their money. There was no way he was going to give up without a fight! He had to think like Troy Randall and come up with some ingenious methods to take out these mechanised menaces. Then Eric had a brilliant brainwave.

He stood and moved to the door, wheeling the teacher's chair along behind him. After lifting the fire extinguisher from the wall, he put it on the chair and returned to the teacher's desk, where he pulled open the drawer and rummaged through the contents. Eventually his fingers fell upon a roll of heavy-duty tape. Without bothering to close the drawer, he returned to the chair.

Standing the heavy extinguisher up, he twisted the nozzle so that it was pointing over the chair's backrest. Next, Eric wrapped the tape around the extinguisher and the back of the chair until it was securely in place. Stepping back, he admired his handiwork.

Moving across the room, Eric began to quietly pull open a series of wooden drawers. Smiling and nodding, he lifted a tub of glass marbles from the third drawer. Returning to the teacher's chair, he placed the tub of marbles on the seat and bound them to the chair with the tape.

Taking a deep breath, Eric placed his hand on the door handle before pulling open the door and making his way into the deserted corridor. Pushing the chair along in front of him, he strained to listen above the noise of the chair's plastic wheels, which squeaked as they moved across the floor.

Eric approached a left turn in the corridor and then paused as a metallic clanking rang out from around the corner. The robot was close. Eric thought back to all of the action movies he'd seen.

The element of surprise was a key tactic and he was now going to use it to his advantage.

Turning the corner with the chair ahead of him, he spotted the robot before it saw him. Reaching over the back of the chair, Eric grabbed the metal pin on the neck of the extinguisher and yanked it free, causing a high-powered jet of gas to noisily rush from the nozzle. He launched the chair towards the robot with as much force as he could muster.

The force of the escaping gas from the fire extinguisher propelled the chair forward at a surprising speed. It hurtled down the narrow corridor, bumping from one wall to the other, but all the time closing in on the robot which had now turned and started to move towards Eric. The gas-powered chair was rocketing along in the robot's direction and it moved like a missile locked on to its target.

The robot detected an imminent problem but couldn't move fast enough. The out-of-control chair collided with the mechanical fiend and knocked it off balance while simultaneously tipping over and scattering the marbles across the corridor floor. The robot teetered and tottered in some sort of crazed robotic dance as it desperately attempted to regain its balance, but it was all to no avail as it slipped and slid on the dozens of marbles.

When the robot finally toppled sideways, it was almost like slow motion. It went over like a freshly felled tree chopped down by a lumberjack and landed on the hard corridor floor with a heavy, metallic thud. The robot's circuitry sparked and crackled as its metal limbs twitched. Eric stood back and waited until it was completely still. The electric blue eyes had gone out, he noticed. "One down," he whispered to himself as he hurriedly made his way past the scene of carnage and headed for cover to buy himself some more thinking time.

Chapter 14

Pushing open the caretaker's office door, Eric stepped inside and closed the door behind him before flicking on the light switch. He grinned as his eyes fell upon a treasure trove of various odds and ends which could prove very useful in his quest to stop the robotic cleaners.

Eric moved to the back of the room and dragged a broken desk to one side, to reveal a rusty old contraption which looked like it hadn't seen the light of day for years. He spat on his finger and rubbed the metal casing to reveal a label which read 'Polish-O-Matic 2000'. He'd found the caretaker's motorised floor polisher! It resembled a large vacuum cleaner and had a huge circular base with a buffing pad underneath. A long metal shaft stuck out of the base and there were levers at the top, plus handlebar controls.

Eric could vaguely remember Mr Summers, the caretaker, perched on the large base unit as he manoeuvred it around the corridors at a surprising speed, buffing and polishing the floors until they were mirror shiny. Unfortunately this was a long time ago and Eric didn't hold out much hope that it still worked. Undaunted, he pulled the rusted machine into a clear space and flicked the power switch on the side.

There was a loud spluttering and clicking before the machine incredibly burst into life. Eric was stunned and delighted and an ingenious idea entered his head. Looking around the room, he spotted a wooden-handled mop propped up in a rusted metal bucket. He tucked the mop under his arm before wedging the door open and clambering onto the motorised floor polisher. Eric pulled the left lever up and the machine lurched forward, causing him to grab for the brake lever. Easing the accelerator lever up again, more carefully this time, he moved out into the corridor. With a turn of the steering bar, Eric set off.

It wasn't long before he came across one of the remaining robots. As he turned onto the main corridor, he came face to face with his next robotic challenge, and grabbed the brake lever to bring the motorised floor polisher to a halt. He waited for the robot to make its move. An eerie silence filled the corridor as the robot waited too. It was like an old-fashioned stand-off in those classic cowboy movies where two gunslingers anxiously faced each other and waited for the other to draw. Eric could feel his heart thumping in his chest and his hands were cold and clammy on the plastic handlebars.

Without warning, the robot set off in Eric's direction, causing him to pull hard on the accelerator lever. The floor polisher burst into life and leapt forward. The Polish-O-Matic's motor roared and whirred as it powered down the corridor with Eric on top. From the opposite direction, the robot bounded along, its metal boots reverberating on the hard floor.

Eric pulled the mop from under his arm and clutched it in his right hand. Like a modern-day knight riding his motorised, floor-polishing steed, he moved at a surprising speed down the corridor towards his opponent. Neither was willing to yield and their head-on charge continued, the distance between them rapidly decreasing. Only a few metres now stood between Eric and his robotic adversary.

Eric pulled the handlebars hard to the left and the floor polisher swerved past the robot as it lunged. Using the wooden point of the mop handle, Eric jabbed with his modern-day jousting lance. He caught the robot in the head with a glancing blow and sent it pirouetting down the corridor. It frantically tried to keep its balance on the freshly polished floor which now resembled a treacherous ice rink.

Eric spun the polisher around just in time to see the robot slide into the wall before slowly turning again, ready for round two. He pulled the accelerator and the floor polisher jerked back into life as Eric began his second charge. The robot was trying to stride out towards him, but was struggling for traction on the freshly polished floor.

This time, Eric took a much firmer grip on the shaft of the mop and pulled the accelerator until his knuckles turned white and he was moving at top speed. The floor polisher's motor loudly hummed as his ride thundered down the corridor and the helpless robot slipped and skidded around, its metal arms outstretched as it tried to stay upright.

Closing his eyes and bracing himself for the final impact, Eric felt a colossal force push against his right arm. It threw him off balance and he was sent cartwheeling up into the air. He landed on the floor before sliding and slithering along the slippery surface, finally coming to a stop in a crumpled heap.

Eric shook his befuddled head and looked down the corridor. The remains of the motorised polisher were lying in a smoking heap. A few feet away, the defeated robot was lifelessly sprawled out on the floor, next to the mop which was now broken and splintered.

Eric cautiously approached his fallen foe. A single wisp of smoke rose from the robot's mouth, but the glowing blue eyes were now no more than two black, lifeless holes. He knelt down and inspected the robot, now reduced to a pile of scrap metal. It looked like the mop had made a direct hit on the main control panel on the front of the robot's chest, dealing it a fatal blow.

Standing up, Eric noticed blood dripping from his left hand. He pulled up his shirt sleeve and jumper to reveal a deep gash on his lower left forearm. It was bleeding profusely and must have occurred during the collision. Eric knew that he had to take cover again and patch himself up. Taking a dirty, crumpled tissue from his trouser pocket, he dabbed at the wound before moving off down the corridor to find a place of safety where he could figure out what to do next.

Chapter 15

Ivana Da Cash moved over to the window and peered out. She could see the flashing blue lights of emergency services vehicles by the school gates. She watched a few policemen, who were milling around and trying to keep a small group of onlookers beyond the hastily assembled police cordon. This was all to be expected, but would not be a problem. Once her demands had been met and the money from the Mayor had been electronically transferred to her account, she would make her escape in her private helicopter which would collect her from the roof. No amount of police cars could stop her then.

Moving back across the hall, she anxiously looked at her watch and noted that the pick-up time was now less than an hour away. She frowned as she pondered the whereabouts of the two robots sent to retrieve the troublesome child who was proving to be a huge hindrance in her otherwise smooth-running plan.

She flicked her finger across the screen of her mobile phone and opened a text message which confirmed the details of her pick-up. In a short while she would be airborne with a cool £1 million in her bank account. Five hours after that, she would be sitting on a golden beach listening to the lapping waves while sipping a delicious cocktail in the glorious sunshine. Ivana smiled at the thought of the warm sun on her face and all that money in her bank account. Her plan was foolproof!

She slid her finger across the phone's screen again, clicked on a number and put the phone to her ear. "Unit 1. Come in, Unit 1." The line crackled but there was no response. Clicking on another number, she again placed the phone to her ear and waited. "Unit 4. Can you hear me, Unit 4? Please respond immediately." The same crackling line met her request.

Frowning, she put the phone in her pocket and made her way to one of the two remaining robots at the back of the hall. Children scooted and scuttled out of her way, making her feel secure in the level of menace and intimidation she held over them. Everyone in the hall feared her and that's how she liked it – they knew she was the boss and nobody would try anything stupid or heroic.

"Unit 3, go out and bring this child in. Find out what's happened to the other robotic units too. I'll not have some snivelling little kid ruining my plan. Go now!" she fiercely commanded.

The robot turned and clanked its way out of the double doors at the rear of the hall as Ivana rubbed her chin in silent contemplation at what may have happened to her two missing robotic sidekicks. Returning to the stage, she picked up the microphone and switched on the speaker system.

Chapter 16

Eric lifted the lid of the plastic first aid box which he'd found in the science room and rifled through the contents. The speaker system suddenly crackled into life.

"Eric Appleby. Eric Appleby. Can you hear me, Eric?" called out a now all-too-familiar voice. "You've had your little bit of fun, but now it's time to play by my rules. I demand that you come to the hall immediately and join the main group. There's a good boy, Eric. My robots are out searching so it'll only be a matter of time before they find you. Better to give up now than force my robots into actions which will definitely be a lot more painful. I really don't want to hurt you, Eric but if you give me no other option, I will." The public address system clicked once and crackled before going silent once more.

Eric processed what he'd heard while he had been unwrapping a long, white bandage from the first aid box. Using his chin to hold one end on the wound on his forearm, he wrapped the bandage round his arm until the deep, bleeding gash was fully covered. He pulled down his shirt and jumper sleeves, and winced at the pain as he sat on one of the wooden stools set out around the room.

There had been four robots to start with, that was something Eric knew for sure. He had taken out two of them already and Ivana Da Cash was not stupid enough to be alone in the hall, so that meant there was one robot searching for him now. Eric pondered the situation and quietly called out to his hero, Troy, for some action hero inspiration. "What would you do if you were in this situation?"

Eric scanned the room and his eyes were drawn to a large tub on the bench at the back, near the door. He walked over and rotated the tub so that he could read the label. In bold, black writing it read 'Plaster of Paris – Fast Setting'. Eric turned the tub again and read the instructions carefully. A crafty idea crept into his head.

He pulled open the door of a cupboard under the bench, and lifted out a red plastic bucket which he half-filled with water from the cold tap at the sink. Taking an empty cup from the drainer, he went back to the Plaster of Paris and placed the bucket of water on the bench next to the tub. Digging the cup into the powder, he scooped out cup after cup and emptied them into the water. He then put the cup on the bench and grabbed a wooden cane propped up against the wall, and stirred the white powder into the water until it began to thicken. Eric then dropped the cane on the floor. He stood on a stool and reached up to balance the bucket on the top of the door.

Carefully slipping out of the classroom through the narrow gap between door and door frame, Eric made his way back out into the corridor. Moving stealthily but at speed, with his back against the wall, he headed along the main corridor in search of the robot which was in turn searching for him. Sooner or later, they would find each other.

It turned out to be a lot quicker than either could have predicted. Turning the corner, Eric spotted the robot slowly cruising down the deserted corridor. "Over here! Hey! Can't you see me?" yelled Eric, waving his arms above his head. The robot stopped and its mechanised head rotated to look at him, its blue eyes blazing in his direction. "Come and get me," goaded Eric as he turned and started to run back the way he'd come. Not waiting for a second invitation, the robot's motorised gear system clicked into life and it began its pursuit.

Feet pounding and heart thumping, Eric charged back to the science room. He loudly banged on a classroom door, the echoing racket leaving the robot in no doubt over which way to go, because being followed was a crucial part of Eric's plan. Behind him, the robot registered the loud thumping and continued its unrelenting pursuit.

Eric slipped back into the science room, taking great care not to disturb the delicately balanced bucket. He didn't have any time to waste.

"I'm in here, you walking pile of scrap metal!" he bellowed through the gap in the door. The robot hurtled towards the classroom.

Eric leapt back just as the robot burst through the door, causing the bucket to tip. The thick paste slithered down the robot's head and oozed over its shoulders and down its arms. The mixture seeped into every nook and cranny. It invaded the creation's inner workings. Thick white blobs dribbled down its metal body and slithered down its legs, making their way into knee and ankle joints. Eric watched as the robot gradually slowed and each movement became more and more difficult. The mixture was rapidly setting and the robot was fast becoming encased in a concrete jacket. The machine was barely able to move and its arms stretched out in fixed positions as it made a desperate attempt to reach out for Eric. It now moved like an old man with chronic arthritis rather than a state-of-the-art piece of robotic technology.

Eventually the machine came to a grinding halt. Eric could hear the inner workings whirring and clicking as it desperately tried to achieve its objective. Then the one blue eye still visible through the white mask flickered and blinked before going out completely. The robot was now no more than a life-size plaster cast model and it no longer posed a threat to Eric.

Eric took a deep breath and gathered his thoughts before sitting down on one of the wooden stools. He wiped his brow with the sleeve of his school jumper as the mummified metal monstrosity vacantly stared at him. "Three down and one to go," he said aloud. "Troy would be proud of me."

Chapter 17

Staring out of the classroom window and across the school car park, Eric could see a heavy police presence outside the school. In addition, there were ambulances and fire engines parked up with their lights flashing. There were groups of adults too, who Eric deduced to be parents, some speaking on mobiles, others tightly clutching their phones as they anxiously awaited news. They all wore the same concerned expressions. Eric couldn't pick out his dad in the throng of people, but he hoped he was out there somewhere.

Large vans with satellite dishes on their roofs were parked along the road and Eric figured they belonged to news crews who had turned up to report on what was taking place. A female news reporter was animatedly speaking to camera. Eric recognised the logos on the broadcast vans were from a prime-time news show – the events at Linkton must have gone global!

High above the school, helicopters noisily

hovered with cameramen desperately trying to get the best footage. Linkton School was clearly making headline news and Eric was caught directly in the eye of a fast-developing and extremely dangerous storm.

As he moved away from the window, Eric pondered his next move. He had one remaining robot to dispatch, then Ivana Da Cash would be alone. His odds had dramatically improved – and so had his self-belief and inner confidence. Eric had transformed into a real-life action hero. The safety of everyone at Linkton depended on his actions and he was determined that he wouldn't let anyone down.

Eric cradled his wounded arm with his right hand as pain surged up to his shoulder and down to his fingertips. The wound burned and throbbed. He needed medical attention but it would have to wait. First, he had some unfinished business to attend to, which required a trip back to the ICT suite. Gritting his teeth and determined to push on through the pain barrier, he headed off.

Chapter 18

Ivana Da Cash removed a laptop from her bag and placed it on the table in front of her. Flipping open the lid, she clicked a series of buttons and moved her outstretched finger across the control pad. Her eyes were fixed on the screen and her focused, professional attitude momentarily slipped as she yelled in delight and punched the air. "I told you there was nothing to worry about," she squealed to her captive audience. "The Mayor of Linkton has done exactly as I requested and my money has been transferred."

"So we can all go free now?" asked Mr Mason, standing up and making his way to the stage.

"Not just yet, my dear Rodney," replied Ivana Da Cash, glancing at her watch as she shut the laptop. "I'll be leaving first, then you lot are free to do whatever you please. My ride out of here is due very shortly. My only regret is that I didn't get to meet the pesky kid who made today so much more difficult than it needed to be." Right on cue, the rear door opened and everyone in the hall turned.

"Eric!" yelled Miss Gregory in a voice tinged with shock and surprise. There, at the back of the hall, was Eric Appleby!

"Didn't want to miss out on all of the fun," said Eric as he confidently made his way down the steps.

Ivana Da Cash's icy glare was filled with equal amounts of hatred and anger. If looks could've killed, it would undoubtedly have finished Eric off there and then. "So we finally meet. You're the troublesome little cockroach who's been the constant pain in my backside," she said. "You could've made all of this so much more straightforward, but instead you wanted to be a hero. Well let me tell you, heroes don't exist. This is real life and the villain wins every time. I'll prove that to you today." Her voice was bitter and acidic as she spat out her words.

Ivana's stiletto shoes made the now all-too-familiar click-clacking noise as she walked down the steps and onto the hall floor. The children sitting close by quickly moved back and a human alleyway was formed. Meanwhile, Eric fearlessly stood his ground. The onlookers watched the confrontation developing before them.

"Well, I think you're wrong," said Eric in a voice filled with self-assurance and newly found confidence.

Nobody in the hall had ever witnessed this side of Eric Appleby before. Miss Gregory stared open-mouthed and Miss Aziz looked on with a quizzical, disbelieving expression. It was as if they were meeting a new pupil for the first time. Gone was the child who desperately lacked self-belief and in his place was a boy who looked like he could take on the world and win!

Ivana Da Cash's body lurched and twitched as she laughed hysterically at the boy's bravado. Then she stopped laughing and glared at Eric with another hate-filled death stare. Turning sharply to the remaining robot standing sentry at the main door, she barked her instructions. "Unit 2, punish this little weasel for his actions today. Make him suffer – lots!" The robot didn't respond. "You stupid hulk of metal! Punish him now! Do as I tell you," ordered Ivana. Still the robot remained rooted to the spot and the woman's instructions continued to fall on deaf ears.

"You need to show a little more respect and use some manners when you speak to people," said Eric in a quiet, controlled voice. He removed a small plastic object that looked like a TV remote from his pocket. "On top of that, make sure that the robotic control system you create can't be hacked. You made it so simple! I just used some of the programming skills taught to me by Miss Aziz to reprogram the last robot." He pointed the object at the robot and pressed one of the buttons. It turned to face him, its blue gleaming eyes shining brightly. "Please stop Ivana Da Cash from escaping," instructed Eric.

Everyone in the hall gasped as the robot clanked towards Ivana, who scampered towards the stage, teetering and tottering on her high heels which were now proving to be a huge hindrance. This was her chance to get to the roof in time for her helicopter collection, but the robot had other ideas.

Throwing the laptop into her bag, she turned towards the exit door leading to the roof – only to be halted in her tracks when the robot clambered onto the stage and reached out a metal arm. Its mechanical hand tightly clamped on to Ivana's right ankle, and dragged her backwards across the stage as she clawed and raked at the wooden surface with her long fingernails.

In one swift movement, the robot lifted her aloft. As she dangled upside down, the pupils and staff erupted into an inferno of cheering and clapping. Some children hugged each other, while others shook their heads in disbelief. Eric walked over to the suspended woman, who was now helplessly thrashing like a fish on a hook. She vainly reached out towards him, her claw-like hands seeking the opportunity to rip him limb from limb.

"I hate you! I'll make you pay for this, just you wait and see," wailed Ivana, who was hanging head first, her long jet-black hair swinging and swaying. "You haven't heard the last of me, Eric Appleby!"

Kneeling down well out of her grabbing range, Eric looked Ivana square in the eye. He smiled at the helpless woman whose face was twisted with fury and rage, anger seeping from every pore. She looked on the verge of passing out. "Seems like you were wrong on both counts. Heroes are very real and, looking at your current situation, the baddie doesn't always win," Eric replied.

He turned to see the staff shepherding the jubilant children towards the exits as police swarmed into the hall.

After a brief conversation with Miss Gregory, a female officer approached Eric. She stared with a stunned expression at the robot which still held Ivana Da Cash aloft. Ivana had now lost any remaining fight and was hanging limply, completely and utterly defeated.

"I think you'd better come with me, Eric Appleby," said the officer as she put her arm around his shoulders. "We'll get that arm checked out by the medical staff and then you can tell me exactly what happened here today."

Epilogue

From that day on, life changed dramatically for Eric Appleby. He became a television regular, chatting to well-known news presenters and doing live interviews for various news channels around the world. He even managed to squeeze in an appearance on The Graham O'Gaunt Chat Show, where he was interviewed about his incredible exploits. The highlight of that appearance was getting to meet his action movie idol, Troy Randall. Eric still has the framed photograph of the two of them on his bedroom wall.

Overnight, Eric was catapulted to superstar status. The huge fees he was paid for sharing his incredible story in the daily newspapers helped to make life easier for him and his dad. Due to his son's popularity, Dad became Eric's agent and gave up his job in the rubber glove factory not long after he'd started it.

People clamoured for Eric's autograph wherever he went and he was forever in demand to pose for a selfie with well-wishers. This happened everywhere from the local fish and chip shop to the Linkton multiplex, where Eric received VIP treatment at the premieres of the latest Hollywood blockbuster action movies. He was even invited to be the guest of honour at the opening of the new supermarket in Linkton. The hero status he'd attained had transformed his life forever, but didn't change him as a person. Eric Appleby remained humble and modest about his death-defying exploits and showed no signs of arrogance or an inflated ego.

As for life at school, that also changed dramatically. Football no longer dominated the conversations, but was replaced by talk of classic action films. Eric could now take part and often held the attention of his classmates by describing both his own exploits as well as those of his action hero, idol and inspiration, Troy Randall. He would leave his peers spellbound and hanging on his every word.

Linkton School eventually returned to normality. A new headteacher was appointed, taking over from the disgraced Rodney Mason who, alongside Ivana Da Cash, was sentenced to a long stretch in prison for their parts in what the media labelled 'The Linkton Siege'. The human cleaners were also reinstated, much to the delight of both staff and pupils. The reappointed cleaning staff worked twice as hard as before, resulting in Linkton School winning the much-coveted 'Cleanest School in Great Britain Award'.

That brings to a close the epic tale of Eric Appleby, the boy whose valiant battle against the dastardly Ivana Da Cash and her fleet of robots saved his school and all those within it and led to his meteoric rise from zero to the most unlikely hero.

Acknowledgements

Thank you to Dad for his advice and support, it's been greatly appreciated and valued. Although Mum hasn't been able to share my writing adventure, I know in my heart that she's been watching over me all the way.

I think the fabulous illustrations in the book really help to bring Eric's story to life. The talented Martin Spore has done a great job and I'd like to thank him for his hard work.

I'd like to thank the fantastic Clare O'Malley who's been an absolute rock. She's been there to share the highs and to provide unwavering support and a reassuring presence during the lows. She really is a diamond!

Huge thanks go to Judy Earnshaw, Susan O'Malley, Jackie Simpson and Phil Whiteley for their constructive feedback and valued advice during the plot and character reads in the early stages of this project. In addition, I'd like to thank Sandra Mangan, Mike and Maggie Barton and

Lesley Bennett for their hard work during the editing and proofing stages of the process.

I would also like to extend my appreciation to Kevin Barber, who has done a fabulous job with the formatting and layout of the interior of the book.

Many more people have been there for me since I embarked on my writing journey and I appreciate the help and support each and every one of them has provided. They're all superstars and I couldn't have done it without them.

A Note From The Author

I hope you enjoyed reading Eric's adventure as much as I enjoyed writing it. Eric Appleby came to life after I combined my love of action movies with my experiences of working in schools. I thought it would be really cool to set an action-packed story in a school and after lots of thinking and planning, Eric's story came to life.

I'm used to writing short stories, as those of you who've read 'Impossible Tales!' will know. I wanted to write a longer story which was a little different and I didn't feel I could do Eric's adventure justice in a short story, so he got a book all of his own. I have the next book mapped out, so please don't think that you've heard the last of Eric Appleby. He'll definitely be back at some point in the future, as will another collection of 'Impossible Tales!'

Until next time though, I hope you read anything you can get your hands on and also keep writing as they are two very important life skills. See you again soon.

Website: www.danworsley.com
Twitter: @dan__worsley

Made in the USA
Charleston, SC
22 November 2015